# jigsaw

For my daughter Morwenna – M.M.

To Christine – T.S.

A TEMPLAR BOOK

Published in the United States in 1997 by The Millbrook Press, Inc.
2 Old New Milford Road, Brookfield, CT 06804

Devised and produced by The Templar Company plc
Pippbrook Mill, London Road, Dorking, Surrey RH4 IJE, Great Britain

Text copyright © 1997 by Miriam Moss
Design and artwork copyright © 1997 by The Templar Company plc

Designed by Mike Jolley

Library of Congress Cataloguing-in-Publication Data
Moss, Miriam.
Jigsaw / written by Miriam Moss ; illustrated by Tony Smith.  p.  cm.
Summary : Provides textual clues in rhyme and progessive visual clues in the form of jigsaw puzzle
pieces to help the reader determine who is creeping through the woods toward a small caped figure lying on the beach.
ISBN 0-7613-0044-9 (lib. bdg.). -- ISBN  0-7613-0074-0 (trade)
I. Toy and movable books -- Specimens.  [I. Mystery and detective stories.  2. Stories in rhyme.  3. Toy and movable books.]
I. Smith, Tony — ill.   II. Title.
PZ8.3.M84665Ji   1997   [E] -- dc20       96-42480   CIP   AC

Printed in Hong Kong

# jigsaw

Written by *Miriam Moss*

Illustrated by *Tony Smith*

THE MILLBROOK PRESS
Brookfield, Connecticut

# In a wood

beneath a hood-

something *stirred.*

# Quite close by

a glistening eye-

spied.

# By a thorny rose

a long sharp nose-

*sniffed.*

# Underneath

grizzly teeth- *grinned.*

# Against a boulder

a heavy shoulder-

*shrugged.*

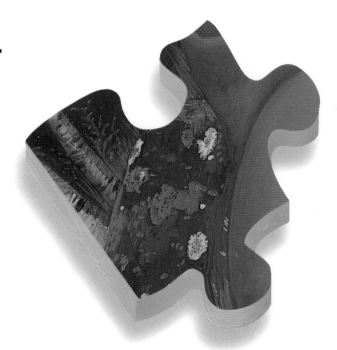

# Beside a tree

a gnarled knee-

*knelt.*

# By a brook

a stockinged foot- *slid*.

# Smooth as an egg

a golden leg-

*lay.*

# Around a chair

a strand of hair-

hooked.

# On
# hairy paws

curled claws-

*closed.*

# On the sand

two small soft hands-

*held...*

*...a jigsaw!*